Young Cam Jansen

and the 100th Day of School Mystery

A Viking Easy-to-Read

BY DAVID A. ADLER

ILLUSTRATED BY SUSANNA NATTI

VIKING

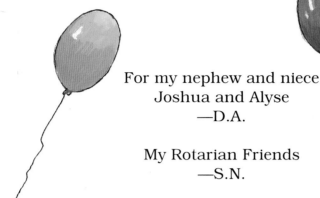

For my nephew and niece
Joshua and Alyse
—D.A.

My Rotarian Friends
—S.N.

VIKING
Published by Penguin Group
Penguin Young Readers Group, 345 Hudson Street, New York, New York 10014, U.S.A.
Penguin Group (Canada), 90 Eglinton Avenue East, Suite 700, Toronto, Ontario, Canada M4P 2Y3
(a division of Pearson Penguin Canada Inc.)
Penguin Books Ltd, 80 Strand, London WC2R 0RL, England
Penguin Ireland, 25 St Stephen's Green, Dublin 2, Ireland (a division of Penguin Books Ltd)
Penguin Group (Australia), 250 Camberwell Road, Camberwell, Victoria 3124, Australia
(a division of Pearson Australia Group Pty Ltd)
Penguin Books India Pvt Ltd, 11 Community Centre, Panchsheel Park, New Delhi – 110 017, India
Penguin Group (NZ), 67 Apollo Drive, Rosedale, North Shore 0632, New Zealand
(a division of Pearson New Zealand Ltd)
Penguin Books (South Africa) (Pty) Ltd, 24 Sturdee Avenue, Rosebank, Johannesburg 2196, South Africa

Penguin Books Ltd, Registered Offices: 80 Strand, London WC2R 0RL, England

First published in 2009 by Viking, a division of Penguin Young Readers Group

3 5 7 9 10 8 6 4

Text copyright © David A. Adler, 2009
Illustrations copyright © Susanna Natti, 2009
All rights reserved.

LIBRARY OF CONGRESS CATALOGING-IN-PUBLICATION DATA IS AVAILABLE
ISBN: 978-0-670-06172-3

Viking® and Easy-to-Read® are registered trademarks of Penguin Group (USA) Inc.

Manufactured in China
Set in Bookman

CONTENTS

1. The *"Click!"* Trick

"Cam! Eric!" Mrs. Wayne called.

"Please, help Maria."

Mrs. Wayne hurried across the hall with Maria.

"These are Cam Jansen and Eric Shelton,"

she told Maria.

"You're in their class."

"Hello," Cam and Eric said.

"This is Maria's first day," Mrs. Wayne said,

"and I have no time to take her to class.

I must get back to the office.

Teachers are waiting to talk to me.

The telephone keeps ringing.

I'm just so busy!"

Cam said, "We'll take her to Ms. Dee's class."

Mrs. Wayne thanked Cam and Eric.

Then she hurried to the office.

"Mrs. Wayne is the principal's secretary,"

Eric said. "She's always busy."

"This may be your first day," Cam told Maria,

"but it's the 100th day for us.

We're having a party."

Cam and Eric took Maria to class.

"Look at all the balloons," Eric said.

"They are all purple or pink

because we're having a Letter P party.

Everything for the party will start with

the letter *P*.

I think we'll be eating pretzels, popcorn,

and maybe pizza."

Cam said, "Kindergarten is having a

Letter A party.

They're having animal crackers and apple juice."

Maria asked, "Why is every class

having a letter party?"

"That was Dr. Prell's idea," Cam said.

"She's the principal, and she loves to read.

Dr. Prell says letters make words.

Words make sentences and stories."

"And that's what we read," Eric said.

"We read stories."

Ms. Dee gave Maria a desk

near Cam, Eric, and Danny.

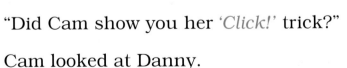

"Hey," Danny said.

"Did Cam show you her *'Click!'* trick?"

Cam looked at Danny.

She said, *"Click!"* and closed her eyes.

"Am I wearing a belt?" Danny asked.

"Yes," Cam answered.

Her eyes were still closed.

"It's blue with pictures of sailboats.

Each sailboat has two red flags."

"How did she remember all that?" Maria asked.

Cam opened her eyes.

Eric told Maria, "Cam has an amazing memory.

It's like she has a camera in her head.

Cam says, *'Click!'* because that's the sound

a camera makes."

Cam's real name is Jennifer.

But when people found out about her great memory, they called her "The Camera."

Soon "The Camera" became just "Cam."

The bell rang.

"Good morning," Dr. Prell said.

She was in her office.

She spoke into a microphone connected to wires and speakers.

Everyone in the school heard her.

"Now please," Dr. Prell said, "stand for the pledge to our flag."

2. Now It's Time to Party

The children stood. They said the pledge.

Dr. Prell made a few more announcements.

Then she said, "Happy 100th day."

"Wow!" Ms. Dee said. "That's a lot of days.

Let's see how much 100 is.

Let's sit quietly for 100 seconds."

Ms. Dee looked at her watch.

The class was quiet.

"Are we done yet?" Danny asked.

"No," Ms. Dee said. "That was just

forty seconds.

We'll start over."

Ms. Dee looked at her watch.

The class was quiet.

Danny looked at Ms. Dee.

He looked at Cam, Eric, and Maria.

He looked at the ceiling.

"That's it," Ms. Dee said at last.

"That was 100 seconds."

"That's all?" Danny said.

"To me, it seemed like a week!"

11

Ms. Dee showed the class pictures
from 100 years ago.

"100 years ago," she said,

"there was no television.

There were no computers and no Internet."

Ms. Dee gave a math lesson on the
number 100.

Then Ms. Dee smiled.

"Now it's time," she said, "for our 100th
day party."

3. No Pizza!

Ms. Dee opened bags of popcorn and pretzels.

She asked Cam, Eric, and Maria

to go to the kitchen

and get the other Letter P foods.

"This is a big school," Eric told Maria.

"But Cam and I know where everything is."

They walked through the cafeteria to the kitchen.

In the kitchen were two boxes.

"There's pizza," Maria said.

"That must be for us."

She opened one of the boxes.

"Hey," she said. "It's not here!"

Cam, Eric, and Maria opened the other box.

It was also empty.

Eric said, "We'll ask Mrs. Apple.

She's the cook. This is her kitchen."

They found Mrs. Apple in the gym teacher's office.

"We're from Ms. Dee's class," Eric said.

"We can't find the pizza."

"They're having a Letter P party,"

Mrs. Apple told Mr. Day, the gym teacher.

"They're having pizza and pineapple juice.

Mr. Baker's class is having a Letter C party.

They're having carrots, cupcakes,

and cherry soda."

Eric said, "The pizza boxes are empty."

"Of course the boxes are empty,"

Mrs. Apple said.

"There are three pizzas warming in the oven."

Cam, Eric, and Maria

followed Mrs. Apple to the kitchen.

Mrs. Apple put on pot-holder gloves.

She opened the oven.

The oven was empty.

4. Who Doesn't Like Noodles and Corn?

Mrs. Apple shook her head.

"I know the pizza was in the oven," she said.

"I put it there."

Mrs. Apple thought for a moment.

"Oh," she said. "Then I took it out

and put it on these racks.

I was waiting for you to pick it up."

The racks were on the counter.

There was no pizza on the racks.

"Could you have put it somewhere else?"

Maria asked.

Mrs. Apple thought for a moment.

"Maybe," she said.

"Lots of times I put things

in the refrigerator or freezer.

Maybe I put the pizza there.

Maybe I put it in the pantry."

Cam opened the refrigerator.

She found pineapple juice, apple juice,

and milk.

Mrs. Apple said, "The apple juice is for

the kindergarten."

Eric opened the freezer.

He found two large containers

of maple walnut ice cream.

Mrs. Apple said, "The maple walnut ice cream

is for Mr. Tate's class.

They're having a Letter M party."

Maria opened the pantry.

She found boxes of noodles

and cans of tomato sauce and corn.

"That's for lunch," Mrs. Apple said.

Maria laughed.

"Now I know who took the pizza," she said.

"It was someone who doesn't like today's lunch.

It was someone who doesn't like

noodles and corn."

5. That's It!

"Everyone likes my lunches," Mrs. Apple said.

Maria said, "Then maybe the gym teacher

ate the pizza. Gym teachers jump a lot.

Jumping would make him hungry."

"No," Mrs. Apple said.

"Mr. Day wouldn't take anything

that wasn't his."

She laughed and said, "And even Mr. Day

couldn't eat all that pizza."

Mrs. Apple opened the refrigerator.

"Take the pineapple juice to your class,"
she said.

"Please, tell Ms. Dee I'm sorry.

I shouldn't have left the kitchen.

Tell her I'll order more pizza."

Cam, Eric, and Maria

each took a can of pineapple juice.

"Cam solves mysteries," Eric told Maria

as they walked to class.

"I bet she'll solve this one

and find the missing pizza."

Cam, Eric, and Maria gave Ms. Dee

the pineapple juice.

Eric told her about the pizza.

Danny gave everyone a paper plate and cup.

Ms. Dee gave them

popcorn, pretzels, and pineapple juice.

Cam nibbled popcorn and looked at Ms. Dee.

She looked at all the letters of the alphabet

on the wall behind Ms. Dee.

"That's it!" Cam said.

She closed her eyes and said, *"Click!"*

Cam looked at a picture she had in her head.

Then Cam opened her eyes and said,

"I know where to find the missing pizza."

6. Messy Pizza

"Where?" Eric asked.

"Yes, where is the pizza?" Maria asked.

"I just hope it hasn't been eaten,"

Cam said.

Cam hurried to the front of the room.

She told Ms. Dee,

"I have to go to Mr. Baker's class.

I think they have our pizza."

Eric and Maria said, "We want to go, too."

Eric and Maria followed Cam out of the room.

Eric asked, "How do you know the pizza is

in Mr. Baker's class?"

Cam stopped.

"What was in the refrigerator?" she asked.

"Cold things," Maria answered.

"Yes," Cam said. "Cold apple juice,

pineapple juice, and milk.

There was apple juice for the Letter A party.

There was pineapple juice for the Letter P party.

There was milk for the Letter M party.

Mr. Baker's class is having a Letter C party.

Where was their cherry soda?"

Eric and Maria shook their heads.

They didn't know.

"The children from Mr. Baker's class

must have already been to the kitchen.

They took the cherry soda.

I think they also took the pizza."

"Why?" Eric asked. "Pizza is a Letter P food."

Cam said, "Mrs. Apple told us there were

three pizzas.

But there were only two pizza boxes.

They must have put the three pizzas into one

of the boxes and taken it to their room."

"But why?" Eric asked again.

"Pizza is a Letter P food."

On Mr. Baker's desk was a pizza box.

"Are you in Ms. Dee's class?"

Mr. Baker asked.

"Yes," Eric told him.

"Then this pizza is yours," Mr. Baker said.

"I was just about to have someone

take it to your room."

More than twenty pizza slices

were jammed in the one pizza box.

Eric took out a slice.

Cheese and tomato sauce dripped off it.

"I'm sorry," Mr. Baker said. "I know it's a mess.

I sent three students to the kitchen.

I said, 'Bring back the Letter C drinks and foods.'

They brought back cupcakes,

cherry soda, and pizza."

Maria said, "But pizza starts with *P*."

"Yes," Cam said. "But cheese begins with *C*,

and pizza has lots of cheese."

Eric went to the kitchen.

He told Mrs. Apple they had found the pizza.

Eric met Cam and Maria in the hall.

He helped them carry the messy box

to Ms. Dee's room.

"Oh, my," Ms. Dee said when she opened it.

"This is a mess!"

She put pizza on a plate.

Danny said, "I'll take that. I like messy food."

Soon everyone in Ms. Dee's class

was eating messy pizza.

Ms. Dee's class had a happy,

messy 100th day party.

A Cam Jansen
Memory Game

Take another look at the picture on page 30.

Study it.

Blink your eyes and say, *"Click!"*

Then turn back to this page

and answer these questions:

1. Is Cam holding a plate of pizza?

2. How many pizza boxes are on Ms. Dee's desk?

3. In the picture, are there more pink balloons or more purple balloons?

4. Is anyone in the picture wearing eyeglasses?

5. What color is Cam's shirt?